Change is scary.

"I kind of like this idea, now that I think on it. Choose a stage name. Be that stage name. See how it goes."

I laugh. "You think I should do it?"

Dr. Steinburg nods. "Really think about the person you want to be, the inner person. And I'm not talking about fame. I'm talking about confidence, grace, poise, passion. Then do the things that such a person would do. I look forward to meeting the person you become."

Strung Out

The String Serial
Part Three

Andrea Ring

Books in
The String Serial

Originally published in 2016 by Square Gorilla Press. For information, visit http://www.squaregorilla.com.

ISBN 978-0692730430

Cover image:

Copyright © 2016 Michael Ring

Cover design:

Hannah Reams, http://www.hannahreams.com

Dedication

To Julie, who has become not only a supporter and a helping hand, but also a friend.

Chapter 1

I don't know why I called my ex-husband. I don't know what I expected from him.

I didn't expect him to show up.

Matt walks in the house with the grace of an athlete and the bulk of a badass. He stops two feet in front of me, and we lock gazes.

"Why did you call me?" he says, and there's not a hint of curiosity in his voice. I can tell he doesn't really care about the why. He just wants an excuse to make a move.

I edge around him and grip the back of the couch for support. "You already know."

He shakes his head. "You need a Scrabble opponent?"

I crack a smile. "I beat you 99% of the time. What fun would that be?"

"So you wanted a little fun?" His eyes seem to darken as he focuses on me and thinks about the fun.

I swallow hard. I didn't think this through.

"We haven't had fun together in a very long time," I say.

"I can fix that," he says, shifting his stance. My eyes dart down to the bulge in his jeans and quickly back up to his face. Is it my imagination, or is the bulge suddenly...bulgier?

"Why are you here?" I ask.

"You called me," he says. "You said you needed me."

I did.

My boyfriend Alec had just texted me all the way from China, telling me not to wait for him. He basically dumped me. And in that moment, with all the pain I felt, I did. I called Matt. I told him I needed him.

"I don't know what I want," I whisper.

Matt laughs. "Join the club."

"So where does that leave us?" I ask.

Matt takes a step toward me. "Are you still seeing that guy? The one you said you loved?"

I shake my head.

"Do you still love him?"

I nod.

"Fuck it," Matt says, and he crosses over to me and crushes his lips to mine.

I close my eyes. I take a deep breath, and Matt's scent—sweet sweat, his aftershave, that funny Irish soap he's used since he was a kid—fills my lungs. Matt. It's so familiar, yet at the same time, I'm a completely different person now than I was when we were married. The last time I kissed him, he was the only man I'd ever been with. The only man I'd ever loved. Now…he's not even the one occupying the most space in my heart.

Tears prick my eyes. My body is responding as though Matt is my one and only. Every cell in my body relaxes as our tongues caress and his hands rub my back. But my heart...it's torn.

I pull back, breathing hard. "Do you think this is a good idea?"

He buries his mouth just below my ear. "We both need it," he says. "Just to see."

"See what?"

He groans against my neck. "Why are you overanalyzing this?"

"Are you going to fuck me and leave?" I ask, and I force myself not to inject even a hint of disapproval in the question. It's just an honest question.

He straightens up and looks me in the eye. "Yes. Because neither of us knows what we want."

I nod. This is true.

Matt takes the nod as an invitation. Before I can blink, my jeans are around my ankles, and I'm draped forward over the arm of the couch, and Matt is fucking me hard. It feels so right, so comfortable, but the tears still spill down my cheeks, and my breath hitches in my throat, and I want to say something, something important, but the words won't come.

But I come. I come in one long, loud scream, and Matt, always the quiet one, groans softly, and then he leans forward and places a tender kiss on my shoulder blade.

"I fucking love you, Hope," he whispers.

My tears speed up, but I force myself not to let him see.

I hear the zipper as Matt fastens his jeans.

I hear the front door close as he leaves.

And I wonder what the fuck I just did.

Chapter 2

Martika hands me a Bloody Mary and pours a glass of straight tomato juice for her pregnant self.

"Since when do you drink tomato juice?" I ask her as I sip.

She shrugs. "My taste buds have a mind of their own. Or my stomach does. I don't even recognize myself right now. I took my bra off last night, and you know what I saw? Little yellow dots on the inside of the cups. I was totally puzzled. Why were there stains on the inside of my bra?"

I raise an eyebrow. "Did you figure it out?"

She nods. "I looked at my nipples, and there was some yellow crust on them. What the hell? So I kind of picked it off, and yellow stuff oozed out."

I laugh. "Serious?"

She laughs, too. "Completely freaked me out. I mean, I knew I was going to breastfeed, and that meant stuff coming out of my nipples, but actually seeing it? Crazy."

I sigh and take a huge swallow of my drink. "I'm never gonna experience that, and I'm starting to think that's not such a bad thing."

Martika sits beside me on the couch and puts a hand on my thigh. "If it'll help, I'll tell you all the awful things about pregnancy. You'll pity me."

I lay my head on her shoulder and sigh again. "So what are you and Benny doing today?"

"Working on the baby's room," she says. "He's freaked out about the baby smelling paint fumes, so he wants to get the painting done today. He read some article that said the fumes need three months to dissipate."

I lift my head and smile. "You're so lucky. He's gonna be a great father."

She rolls her eyes. "Not that I disagree, but the master sergeant in him has kicked in. He's making lists. He hired some safety guru to come in and baby-proof the house."

"I didn't know that was an actual job," I say.

She nods. "A thousand bucks for something we can do ourselves for a hundred. And he's researching bottles and nipples. Some of the cheap brands apparently have cancer-causing chemicals in the latex. Not to mention that babies can be allergic to latex."

I smile. "This is kind of perfect. Since I saw you unearth a Skittle from your couch cushions last week and pop it into your mouth, I'm thinking you'll balance each other out."

Martika laughs. "Yep. The five-second rule is one I live by. Unless there's sugar involved. Then it's more like a five-month rule. So what does your mom have planned today?"

According to my mother's therapy, we spend Sundays together. My mother usually dictates the activity.

"Yoga," I say. "She's been trying to get me to go for years. I agreed with the stipulation that I get a cheeseburger afterward."

"That explains the Bloody Mary," she says. "Need another?"

ॐ

So mid-morning yoga at The Enlightened Soul. My mother made me buy a mat, one of those squishy things that's not actually comfortable on a hard floor, and I tried it out last night. I spent two hours brushing all the dirt off the bottom (and I thought my house was clean!). Apparently, every little hair and speck of dust sticks to these damn things.

My mat is purple with swirly yellow flowers all over it—yay! But when I meet my mother in the parking lot, she looks at my mat and grimaces.

"What did you buy?" she asks.

"Isn't it purdy?" I say. "And it was on sale."

"That's because no one who actually does yoga would buy it," she says. "It doesn't even have any grip marks. It's like a slip 'n slide."

I grit my teeth. "Do you have to criticize every little thing? Why didn't you tell me I needed a mat with grip marks?"

Andrea Ring

She starts to walk toward the studio entrance, and I'm forced to follow. "I didn't know they made them without them. Why didn't you buy one here, like I told you to?"

"Because they're $54 here," I say. "I'm not spending $54 for one hour of my life."

"So you're already assuming you won't be back," she says. "Honestly, Hope, you need to have a better attitude." She pulls on the door and holds it open for me. I ignore her and walk in.

Gah. It's like a hundred degrees in here. I can feel the sweat oozing from my armpits already.

My mother grabs my arm as she marches to the middle of the room and forcibly positions me to her right.

"Shoes and socks against that wall. Then we meditate until we start," she says.

"Um…can't I keep my socks on?" I ask.

"No."

She rolls out her plain blue mat, strips off her shoes and socks, and deposits them against the wall. Then she sits on her mat in the lotus position. Her eyes close and the wrinkles of disapproval around her mouth relax.

Fine. I roll out my mat and take off my shoes. My socks…good Lord, I didn't know I'd have to be barefoot. I haven't actually painted my toes in a month. Chipped bits of Purple Orchid polish dot my toenails, which also look a bit long. Christ. I try to hide my toes by curling them and limp to the wall to deposit my shoes. Then I run back and sit down.

My knee pops. I grab my left ankle and drag it up tight against my inner right thigh. Yow. That actually hurts.

Now my right ankle. *Owwie, owwie, owwie!* I cry in my head as I get into position. How can anyone relax while their thighs are screaming at them? The toenail on my big toe digs into my calf and draws blood.

"Welcome, friends," the instructor says. "Rosalyn, I see you've brought someone. Finally. You must be Hope?"

I smile at her. "Yep. I'm Hope. Hello."

"Have you done any yoga before?" she asks.

"No," I say. "This is my first time."

Someone behind me snickers.

"I'm sure Rosalyn told you, but this an advanced class, so just do what you're comfortable with. If there's a pose you're having trouble with, don't push it. Just do what you can."

I nod. "I will, thanks."

"Okay," she says. "Let's start by getting on all fours, breathing deep, relaxing our neck, and drop to a Downward Dog."

"Did she say dog?" I ask a little too loudly.

"Don't talk," my mother whispers. "Just do it."

I try to copy what everyone around me is doing. But of course, when I drop my head, I can't see shit. Plus, the blood rushes to my head and makes me dizzy. I spend the first twenty minutes with my neck craned at awkward angles, trying to open up my hips (whatever that means), and sliding into a cobra. Which is kind of fun, I admit. I can slither. But my arms aren't strong enough to hold a plank position and lower myself down. I thud to the mat ungracefully before every slither.

"Now lift your leg up," the instructor says, "then curl it back, open up the hips, make room for your neck, make sure it's relaxed…"

My leg flails up. My arms shake. I try to curl my leg back, and I topple over to my left and crash into my mother.

"Ooph," she says from underneath me.

The instructor rushes over to us and helps me roll off Mom. "Are you hurt?" she asks.

"My leg just got a little excited," I say. "We're fine."

"Speak for yourself," my mother says. "I'm bleeding."

We both look at Mom. She has a cut on her cheek.

"How'd you do that?" I ask.

She glares at me. "Your toenail."

ʋ

I slide into the booth across from my mother. The cut on her cheek has at least stopped bleeding.

"Her beginning classes are quite good," my mother says after we order lunch. "You need strength training. Your arms are like rubber bands."

"I'm not going back there," I say. "It was humiliating."

"It's not my fault you don't exercise," she says.

"It's your fault I tried a handstand," I say. "I can't do a push-up. What made you think I could do a handstand?"

"You have to try to succeed," she says. "Yes, you'll fail a million times. But the million and first, you won't. That's the point."

"Poor Howard," I say, referring to the man on my right in the yoga class. "I hope the swelling goes down quickly."

"It's not Howard's first yoga accident," she says. "He'll be fine. But maybe you should bring him a bottle of scotch next Sunday. As a peace offering."

"I'm not going back," I repeat.

Mom just smiles. "We'll see."

Chapter 3

Dr. Steinburg's office is colder than usual. Or maybe it's just that my body has the permanent shakes since that night with Matt.

"So how goes the love?" my therapist asks me as I take my regular seat. My eyes sting, but I'm determined not to cry.

"Well...Alec had some emergency and had to go to China for an indeterminate amount of time. So he told me not to wait for him."

Dr. Steinburg raises an eyebrow. "Did he say why he left?"

"No," I say. "Just that his life was about to change, and he couldn't put me through that, so that's it."

"Are you alright, Hope?" he asks.

I shake my head. "Not really. And I'm so not alright that I slept with Matt."

He shifts in his chair. "Are you seeing him?"

"No. He's been showing up, and saying he's confused, and I've been fighting him off. But when Alec told me to get lost...I instigated it. I called Matt."

"And what were you hoping to get out of that call?" he asks.

I shrug. "Company. Commiseration. Empathy. I just didn't want to be alone."

"But you could have called Martika," he says. "Or your mother."

I nod. I could have.

Should have.

"And how did you and Matt leave things?"

"The same," I say. "We both acknowledged we don't know what we want. It was a moment of weakness."

Dr. Steinburg nods. "Weakness, yes, but also immaturity. You ran back to the familiar without thinking about the consequences."

"Probably," I say. I don't really want to discuss it.

Dr. Steinburg reads me perfectly and changes the subject. "What's going on with your music?"

"I had a meeting with Lockstep Records," I say. "But they're jerks. I've been writing some new songs, and I was thinking about just starting my own thing. Maybe using a fake name."

"What's wrong with your real name?"

I glare at him. "You already know."

"So you're choosing the most difficult path just because you don't want to give your dead father the satisfaction of knowing his name opened doors?"

"I can do it on my own," I say. "And I can be anyone I want to be."

"Besides your name," he says, "and besides your father, what's so awful about being Hope Cruz Russell?"

"Nothing," I say. "I mean, it's not that."

"Isn't it?"

My eyes find my lap. I can't make myself look up. "I want to live long enough to grow old with someone. I want to have confidence. I want to take advantage of every minute I have left and make my mark on the world. That's…"

I finally raise my eyes. Dr. Steinburg is staring at me patiently.

"That's the one thing my dad taught me. He grabbed life by the balls. He didn't let anything stand in his way. He told the world to listen up or fuck off."

"So what is stopping you from doing the same?" he asks.

I sigh. "I'm just not that kind of person. I'm quiet and shy, and I have trouble with crowds, and I just think that maybe if I created a new persona, it would be easier."

"You know, the only way to change our inner selves is through our behavior. Oh, you'll hear all this crap about positive thinking and imagining yourself doing what you want to do, but imagining gets us nowhere. You want to be outgoing? Then be outgoing. You want the world to listen up? Then you have to tell them to listen up. And then your actions will change your emotions. They will change your thinking. You will become that which you do. We are our actions."

"You make it sound easy," I say.

"Easy? No. But it is quite simple. I kind of like this idea, now that I think on it. Choose a stage name. Be that stage name. See how it goes."

I laugh. "You think I should do it?"

Dr. Steinburg nods. "Really think about the person you want to be, the inner person. And I'm not talking about fame. I'm talking about confidence, grace, poise, passion. Then do the things that such a person would do. I look forward to meeting the person you become."

ഐ

I get home and open my laptop.

I already know who I want to be. I just need to be her.

I order six wigs and ten new pairs of sunglasses off Amazon. I buy a leather biker jacket with a gold zipper. I buy a white pair of leather creepers that I've always wanted but was too much of a pussy to buy. I buy a knee-high pair of purple combat boots. Who knows how I'll wear all this stuff, but I like it. It feels like me.

The new me.

Lady Strings.

Here I am.

Chapter 4

It's open-mike night at The Ugly Mug in Old Towne Orange, and you have to sign up in advance to play. I liked the idea of that—I'm committed. If I'd just had to show up, I might have chickened out.

Or maybe not. I like the playing music part. It's the "act like a rock star" part I'm not so good at.

Martika and Benny are coming tonight to offer some support. According to Martika, they'll be the crowd exciters. No musician wants to play to a sedate crowd, and Martika knows how to be loud.

So I've got on my platinum blonde bob wig, oversized black sunglasses ala Jackie O, a tight black top that shows off my boobs under my leather jacket, and my purple combat boots. I look ready, even if I don't feel ready.

I get one song, more if the audience responds. Fingers crossed that they respond.

The place is packed when I enter, but I spot Marti and Ben right away. They snagged the front-and-center table. Typical. So I check in with the staff and then squat down next to Martika.

"What do you think?" I whisper to her.

She glances down at me and leans away. "If you're playing tonight, I hope you go first. 'Cause once Lady Strings comes on, she's not leaving the stage."

I cock my head. "She's that good, huh?" I can't keep the laughter out of my voice, and Martika's mouth drops open.

"Hope?"

I nod.

Martika squeals and throws her arm around my shoulder, squeezing my neck tight. "Oh my God, you look incredible! I didn't know it was you!"

"Shhh," I say. "That's the point."

She releases me with a smile. "Knock 'em dead, kid."

Benny smiles and gives me a thumbs up.

I stand up and lean against the wall near the back. There aren't any open seats anyway, and this way I get a good view of the crowd and can gauge their reactions.

The first musician to come on is a greasy guy, mid-twenties, with hair down to his butt and a Ron Jeremy mustache. He looks like a transplant from the seventies.

And that's pretty much what he is, as he sings "Hot Blooded" by Foreigner, butchering every note. The audience cringes every time he goes into the chorus. But he's enthusiastic, I'll give him that. He's strutting his stuff, bending over the mike stand and closing his eyes as he sings the high notes. He looks the part.

He gets tepid applause at the end, and lots of cheers from a table in the middle. He grins to his buddies, and sits on a girl's lap.

Next up is a college girl in a floral sundress. Hello, it's the beginning of February. She sings a Fall Out Boy song, has a decent voice, but is wobbly with nerves. Seems like she lost a bet or took up a challenge from her sorority sisters. Either way, she gets some genuine applause and some cheers of encouragement, but not enough to warrant an encore.

My turn.

I pull a stool up to the microphone and adjust the stand. I get a few whistles, and a "Yeah, Baby!" from the frat boys at the back. I grin.

"My name is Lady Strings, and I'm thrilled to be here tonight. Sing along if you know this one."

Martika gives a loud "Whooo!" Ben gives a "Yeah!"

Then I tap the flat of my hand on the guitar four times and play a stripped-down version of Britney Spears' "Hit Me Baby One More Time."

It takes the first verse before people recognize the song. Everyone's staring at me slightly open-mouthed, and I see the moment when that recognition hits—people lean in to their neighbors, whisper, I get a few hoots, and toes start tapping.

By the second verse, everyone's singing with me, and Martika gets to her feet and starts clapping in rhythm over her head.

Ben joins her.

And then, I don't know, maybe the people behind them just can't see me anymore and want a better view, but they stand up. The sorority girls get to their feet giggling, belting out the lyrics. The frat boys move closer to them. I crook my finger at the girl in the floral sundress, and she mouths, "Me?" and I nod, and she comes to stand next to me, and we sing together.

And when I finish, the place goes wild. People are stamping their feet and cheering, and the applause shakes the rafters. I laugh and stand up for a bow.

"You're really great," Sundress Girl says. I slip my sunglasses down just enough to show my eyes, and I give her a wink.

"Another one!" Martika yells. "We want more!"

I look up at the manager of the coffeehouse and cock my head. He nods at me, so I sit back down on the stool.

"Wow, thank you," I say. "Thank you so much. Okay. Let's do another."

So I play "Personal Jesus" by Depeche Mode. Even the younger kids in the crowd know this song. Martika leads the way, clapping hard as a substitute for drums. The crowd joins in, and we rock.

I follow that with one of my original songs, and end with "The Scientist" by Coldplay.

After, I'm mobbed, and I give out all the USB sticks I'd brought with six of my songs on each. Martika drags out her iPad, and gets people to sign up for my exclusive mailing list. I book the next four Wednesday nights at The Ugly Mug.

When I finish my free latte and stand to leave with Martika and Benny, my eyes go to the door. I see the back of Matt as he slips out without a word.

Chapter 5

"This is becoming a habit," I say as I exit my car and spy Matt on my front steps. "Maybe I should put out a lounge chair for you."

He stands. "I saw you tonight."

I don't say anything.

"Why are you wearing a wig?"

"You don't like me as a blonde?" I ask.

Matt shakes his head. "It's fine. It's just not you."

"Maybe you don't know me," I say. I head past him to the door, and Matt pulls on my arm.

"Are you afraid to be you?"

"I'm not afraid of anything, Matt," I say. "I'm just trying to play my music without my dad involved."

He takes his hand away and stuffs it in his pocket. "People will find out eventually. Isn't it exhausting, trying to be somebody you're not?"

"It was one performance," I say, "at a little nothing coffee shop. I'm not in danger of exhausting myself over one performance."

"What's wrong with Hope Russell?" he says. "You don't have to do this."

"You found plenty wrong with Hope Russell, if memory serves," I say.

Matt growls in frustration. "It wasn't about you, okay? The whole thing was about me. I was the failure! I was the one who couldn't help you! Do you know what that's like? Waking up every day and feeling like you're worthless?"

I just stare at him. Yep, I know something about that.

"I fucked that grad student not because I loved her, not even because I liked her. I just needed to feel like I was good at something. She looked up to me in the department, and she thought I was successful, and...I just needed that feeling."

"I'm so sorry," I say. I bow my head. "I'm sorry I didn't give you that. I never thought of you as a failure."

"Christ, don't apologize!" he screams. "I'm the fuck-up."

"You are," I say. "But I'm still sorry."

Matt huffs a breath and smiles. "You're the only thing that's ever mattered to me. Your health, your happiness...that's all I ever wanted."

"I'm healthy now. And happy. At least, happier than I've ever been."

He flinches at that. "Really? You're happier than when we were married?"

"With myself," I say. "My state of mind. Looking back...I thought I was happy at the time, but now that I'm facing stuff and being honest with myself...we were going through the motions, Matt.

I didn't even know what love and sacrifice meant. Happiness was the absence of conflict. And that's not real happiness."

"You're right," he says. "We weren't happy. But that doesn't mean things couldn't be different."

"I'm not ready," I say. "I'm not ready to jump into that comfortable place. What if nothing changes?"

"We won't know that unless we try."

I scuff my boot over the concrete. "Maybe we could try being friends."

Matt grins. "With benefits?"

I shake my head. "No benefits. Just friends."

The smile slips from his lips, but he nods. "I'd like that."

He moves to stand in front of me. My body trembles at the closeness as he leans into me. And then he plants a very soft, sweet kiss on my cheek.

"I was proud of you tonight," he whispers. And then he walks to his car.

Chapter 6

My mother and I meet with Alice Wills, our new attorney who's looking into the shady dealings of our former attorneys who handled the music rights for my dad's catalog. Alice waves us each to a seat and takes the great big leather chair behind her desk.

"So," she says. "Looks like Mayberry & Foster did indeed close the Spotify deal, the *Cop Killer Reloaded* video game deal, and the one with the senator's campaign. I have the contracts here." She hands us each a stack of papers.

I immediately flip to the signature pages.

"That's my signature," I say, "but I absolutely did not sign these."

"I know," she says. "They're forged. I have a handwriting expert who can pick out the little details. But we also just received the accounting report, and everything's on the up and up. Even though you didn't sign these contracts, the monies are in your escrow account at the firm. And they've accumulated a nice bit of interest."

"Are you saying that we need to suck it up because they didn't steal any money?" my mother shrieks.

"No," Alice says patiently. "What I'm saying is that we have to prove damages. You don't have any financial damages, so we then look at damage to the estate's reputation. Obviously…it's a gray area."

"Doesn't look gray to me," Mom says. "That video game promotes violence. We don't condone that."

Alice nods. "Yes…but the jury's not going to look at your background, Mrs. Cruz. It is your husband's character that will be on trial. It's common knowledge that he died of a drug overdose and that he was arrested for assault on numerous occasions. Is there something in his past that would indicate he'd be against these things today?"

"Just because he was an ass doesn't mean he'd want to profit off all his bad behavior," Mom says stubbornly.

"But Mayberry & Foster will make exactly that case," Alice says. "Look, they did something that is absolutely wrong and illegal. And we'll make them pay for that. But I don't want this case to go to trial. Besides dragging you two through the mud, a jury trial is just plain unpredictable. We can probably fill the jury with people sympathetic to your stance on the video game, and even Senator Horton's legalize-all-drugs campaign. But the subscription service deal is dicey. People are starting to believe that information should be widely available and even free. People want to hear Joe Cruz's music, and right now, they can't unless they buy it the old fashioned way or steal it."

"It isn't even about the specific deals, is it?" I ask. "It's the fact that they forged our signatures and profited off of something they had no right to."

"That's exactly what we'll focus on as we negotiate a settlement," Alice says. "But in a jury trial, they'll try to obscure their guilt using any means possible."

"I want those attorneys fired," Mom says. "That's non-negotiable. I want them disbarred."

"That's really what this is about," I say. "You know we don't need some huge amount of money. Whatever we get will go to charity. We just want justice."

Alice closes the file in front of her and grins. "Justice is what I do."

☙

I sit down with my laptop after dinner, and my hands itch. I want to write a letter to the editor of the LA Times, telling the world about my scumbag lawyers. I want to rip them apart on Yelp. Or post a picture of the douchebag attorney Alan with a mustache and horns and a one-inch dick hanging out of his pants.

But I can't. I can't say a word about any of it, or they can turn around and sue me.

A text distracts me. Chet, the son of one of my mother's ex-boyfriends. *Come have a beer with us.*

I smile and answer back. *Where?*

Gino's. We're at the bar. Huuuurrrrry!!!

Ahh. It's kind of nice for someone to want my company that much.

I exchange my wool pants for jeans, my heels for the creepers. Throw on the leather jacket and some shiny green eyeshadow.

Chet is leaning on the arm of Clancy, his better half, who's gesticulating to a group of men leaning on the bar. I hug Chet from behind and kiss his shoulder. "I've missed you," I say.

He turns around and smiles, bestowing my cheek with a kiss. "Ditto. I thought a night of debauchery with us was preferable to a night of moping at home alone. What are you wearing?"

I spin around. "You like? It's my new look."

"I like," Clancy says, pulling me into a hug. "But your poor hair."

I shrug and run a hand over the back of my head, which still bears the scar of an unfortunate head injury. "Nothing to be done unless I want to shave it all," I say.

"Excellent," Clancy says. "I have an electric razor at home. If you pay me in tequila, I'll do it."

I laugh. "I'm not shaving my head. And if I were, I wouldn't let a drunk lawyer do it."

Clancy holds out his hand and spreads his fingers. "Look at me. Not a shake. I'm solid as a rock."

Chet waves a hand. "Clancy has no idea what he's doing, it's true. But this is a good idea. Why don't you cut your hair?"

Those words sound foreign to me. "Cut my hair? No way. I've always had it long."

Chet lifts my hair up off my neck and kind of tucks the ends under. "Cute. It'd be so cute! And you can dye it. Maybe pink?"

"Lavender," Clancy says. "That lavender gray that's so popular right now. Damn, that would be hot."

I laugh again. "I just bought a bunch of wigs. I think those are a safer bet."

"I saw the video," Chet says. "The bob was great, but the blonde washed you out."

"Gee, thanks," I say.

He smiles. "If you're wearing wigs, then who cares what your real hair looks like? Live a little!"

"I'll think about it," I say. "Now buy me a drink."

"Ooh, the lady's feisty tonight," Clancy says. He pulls on the shirt of the guy standing next to him. "Logan, you're into feisty ladies."

Logan turns and gives me a smile. He reminds me of the Marlboro man—tall, beefy, rugged. Not classically handsome, but definitely sexy and all male.

I hold out my hand. "I'm Hope."

"Hope," he says, shaking my hand firmly. "Logan. Clancy and I are neighbors."

"Ah," I say. "What do you do, Logan?"

"He's a firefighter," Chet whispers loudly. Then he giggles.

I laugh. "Looks like he's good at lighting the fires. I wonder how good he is at quenching them."

Chet and Logan laugh, and Clancy rolls his eyes. "That's the best line you can come up with? 'He's good at lighting fires?'"

"You've got a better one?" I challenge.

Clancy smiles. "I bet he has the longest hose here. And if you want him to put out the fire, just stop, drop, and roll."

We all laugh, and then I look at Logan. "You heard those before?"

Logan grins. "My favorite is, wanna slide down my pole?"

I roll my eyes. "That's never actually worked, has it?"

"I don't know," he says. "But it looks promising so far."

Chet puts an arm around my shoulder. "I'm sorry, Logan, but Hope's off limits. She wants an actual commitment."

"Doesn't mean I can't flirt," I say.

"Fine," Chet says, "but no sex!"

"What are you, my mother?"

Chet looks at me, dead-pan. "Funny."

"I can have sex if I want," I say, "but I need a few drinks first."

Logan signals the bartender.

ಐ

My only excuse is that...let's face it. I have no excuse. I'm at the bar with a bunch of horny men and I'm wasted.

But at least I know I'm wasted. That has to count for something.

We all climb in a cab and head to Clancy's. But as we pass a drugstore, Clancy orders the cab driver to stop and wait. Five minutes later, he's back in the car, his purchase tucked under his shirt. Despite Chet's ribbing, Clancy won't tell us what he bought.

Inside his apartment, I start to sweat. "Is it hot in here?"

Logan puts his hands on my waist. "With you in here, it is."

I laugh. That's like the funniest thing I've ever heard.

I unzip my jacket and throw it on the couch. The men all gape at me. "What?"

"Oh, dear," Chet says, shaking his head. "I'm not being a very good friend tonight, am I?"

I crease my brow and take his hands in mine. "Don't say that. You're the best friend anyone could have! Absolutely the best!" I squeeze his hands tight, and in my drunken fog, I nod twice for emphasis.

Chet smiles. "I'm supposed to be protecting you. Come on, love. Put this on." He starts to unbutton his shirt.

"Why do you want me to wear your shirt?" I ask.

He shrugs off the shirt and puts my arms in the sleeves. "Because all you have on is a bra."

I look down at my chest. Hello, wow. There are my boobs. "Oh."

He pulls the shirt into place and buttons two buttons. "I'll have Clancy drive you home. I didn't realize you were this knackered."

"Knackered?" I say with a giggle. "Channeling your English forebears, are you?"

"Knackered is good," Clancy says. He pulls out the bag from underneath his shirt. "We're going to color your hair!"

I squeal. "Oh, goody! Did you get the lavender?"

"Not that much choice on a Saturday night," he says. "I have one box of bleach to strip the color from your hair, and then we're going...wait for it...blue!"

I gasp. Blue! How exciting!

Logan laughs. "You should probably remove that shirt. You don't want to get it all blue."

I totally agree. "Yeah, Chet. This shirt is expensive." I take it off and throw it on the floor.

Chet sighs. "Logan, my dear, I think it's time for you to go."

"But—"

"No buts," Chet says, steering him to the door. "Show's over."

"Call me!" I yell at Logan. "I'll miss you!"

Logan laughs and out he goes.

ဆ

I wake up on Clancy's couch, and I'm amazed I don't have a hangover. And then I sit up. Ugh. I feel like a dry loofah. I need water.

I go to the kitchen and fill a glass from the tap. I down it. Then I get another.

"Morning, sexy," Clancy says at my back. I turn and smile.

"Morning. Sorry about last night."

He kisses my cheek. "Sorry for what?"

"Drinking so much," I say. "I was a little out of it."

Clancy leans back against the counter and raises an eyebrow. "You don't get out much, do you?"

"Not much," I admit. "But still…thanks for taking care of me."

Chet comes in wearing only boxers. "You haven't seen your hair yet, have you?"

My hand automatically flies to my head. I pat it. Sweet Jesus, my hair is practically gone!

I run to the bathroom and flip on the light. I just stare.

"Lady Strings," Clancy says behind me. "Ta da!"

My hair is about two inches long. All over. Sticking up in every direction. And it's a bright cobalt blue.

Chet hugs me from the back. "Remember, you have wigs. It's only hair. It grows."

My eyes sting. "If I hadn't been wasted last night, I...I never would have done this."

Chet squeezes me harder.

I turn in his arms and look at Clancy. He just stares at me uncertainly.

Then I launch myself at him and crush him in a hug.

"Thank you," I whisper. "Thank you. I never would have had the courage to do this on my own."

In the mirror behind him, I see Clancy smile at Chet. Chet swipes his hand over his brow.

Chapter 7

My phone rings as I'm trying to knit a baby blanket for Martika. I throw my needles beside me and answer the unfamiliar number.

"Hello?"

"Hey, Hope. It's Logan. The firefighter from last night?"

I laugh. "I remember. I wasn't that drunk."

"Were you drunk enough to let Clancy dye your hair?"

I laugh again. "Well, you got me there. How are you?"

"Good," he says. "I have tonight off, and I thought maybe we could hang out."

"Sounds like fun. What did you have in mind?"

"Some of the guys I work with are meeting for drinks," he says. "At the Brewing Company on Newport. I can pick you up. Say, 7?"

Another night of drinking. Just what I don't need.

"Great!" I hear myself say.

❧

Logan introduces me to his friends, and wow. Okay, not all of them have the face of a god, but their bodies? Make me want to light my house on fire just to have them come rescue me.

Logan buys me a pear cider without asking me. Whoa, it's kind of yummy. I know I should probably exercise my new-found voice and object, but he seems pleased with himself. No need to ruin the mood.

"Have you always had blue hair?" Fireman Aidan asks me. Logan has wandered down the bar, talking to some girl he knows. At least his buddies aren't that rude.

"I just dyed it last night," I say. "Kind of a spur-of-the-moment decision."

"That takes balls," he says. "Or have you always been that bold?"

I shake my head. "I was a little drunk," I admit. "Not as ballsy as you think."

He grins and looks down at Logan, then back at me. "How do you know Logan?"

"I'm friends with his neighbor. Just met him last night."

"And you agreed that fast, huh?"

I crease my brow. "You mean agreed to hang out?"

Aidan laughs. "Is that what we're calling it?"

"I don't follow."

"I mean the after part," he says. "Have you done it before?"

Andrea Ring

I'm thoroughly confused. "What after part?"

Aidan frowns. "You mean, he didn't tell you?"

"Tell me what?"

He looks suspicious, like I'm just playing dumb. "You're coming back to my place after this. Right?"

I glance down at Logan. He notices me and gives a little smile. "Logan didn't mention that."

Aidan scrubs a hand through his hair. "Shit. Sorry. I thought he talked to you—"

"About what?"

"Well…he said he was bringing the girl. I assumed it was you."

I slug back my cider. "Bringing the girl for what?"

Aidan leans in a little closer to me. "For a threesome. It's fun as hell. You should think about it."

I pause with my glass at my lips. "You want to have a threesome with me and Logan?"

"You're sexy," he says, lowering his voice. "We'll take care of you."

Uh…what? That's not happening. Not in a thousand years. But I don't say that out loud.

"And you're okay with another guy?" I ask. "I mean, I can understand the appeal of having two girls, but…another guy?"

He shrugs. "Don't knock it 'til you try it. It's fun to watch."

I nod slowly. "And do you and Logan…touch each other?"

Aidan smiles. "If the lady wants us to."

Okay, so my nipples harden at that. I have no idea why. I've never even thought about this stuff. But that doesn't mean I'm gonna do it.

"And how many ladies have you done this with?" I ask.

"A few," he says. "It's not always easy to find a willing participant, but you'd be amazed how many people are into it."

Yes, I would.

I look into my glass. The cider's almost gone, and my head is swimming. Now I know why Logan ordered it—it's twice as powerful as a glass of beer. Guess I gave him the wrong impression last night.

"So I guess you don't have a girlfriend," I say.

"I used to," he says. "Just broke up two weeks ago."

"I'm guessing your lifestyle would be tough for a girlfriend."

He laughs. "She got me into it."

Ooo-kay. I clearly need to get out more.

I rummage in my purse and pull out a ten-dollar bill. I throw it on the bar.

"Tell Logan I paid for my own drink," I say. I slide off the bar stool, and Aidan puts his hand on my arm.

"You're leaving?"

"Tell him I was gonna make him scream tonight," I say. "I was gonna suck his cock so hard he'd be seeing stars. But since he can't even be bothered to talk to me...fuck him."

Aidan's eyes go wide. "We can leave him here. We don't need him. We can go to my place."

I put my hand on his cheek. "I'm sorry, Aidan. You seem like a decent guy. But I only fuck people I'm attracted to."

And I head out the door.

Chapter 8

Martika laughs hysterically as I tell her about my "date" with Logan.

"Finally," she says. "You finally had a date with an asshole."

"What's that supposed to mean?" I ask.

"I've been amazed at all these guys," she says. "You've met one nice guy after another. Statistically, you were due for a clunker."

I laugh. "I guess you're right."

"You're coming to my Lamaze class tomorrow night, right?" she asks.

"Yep. I'll be there."

"Benny's pouting," she says. "He doesn't want to miss it."

I shake my head. "I'd think he'd be glad. Isn't it boring for most guys?"

"Benny's not most guys."

"True," I say. "Okay, I'll see you tomorrow."

❧

So Lamaze class. I don't know anything about Lamaze. I only know that when you're pregnant, you learn to do it. It's some kind of birthing technique, I think.

Martika signed up for a six-week class, and I'm glad I'm here on night one. Everyone in the room is as clueless as me.

The class is at St. Joseph's Hospital, in one of their teaching rooms. I didn't know hospitals have classrooms. Learn something every day.

We all sit on the floor in front of a projector screen, and I'm irritated immediately. Some of these women look ready to pop. I wonder how the hell they'll get back on their feet.

The instructor starts talking, and I glance around. Yikes. The lady sitting next to me has purple feet so swollen they look like they belong on an elephant. Poor thing. The woman next to her has a shirt on that's so tight it looks like the sleeves are cutting off the circulation in her arms. They all look happy, though. Even if they're bloated.

The lights go out, and a movie comes on, and I realize I haven't been paying attention at all. I lean into Martika's ear. "What's this about?"

"It's a live birth," she whispers back. "Just close your eyes if you need to."

Birth doesn't bother me. At least, I don't think it does. Only violence and blood bother me. I should be good.

We watch a doctor check the woman to see how much her cervix has dilated. Huh. The doctor figures this out with his fingers?

"Ten centimeters," he says. "You're ready to push."

The woman is doing some funny breathing stuff, panting like she's a banshee. Her partner bathes her brow and massages her shoulders. Wow. It looks like she's in a lot of pain.

The camera perspective changes. Now we're getting a full-on shot of her hairy hoo-hah. The woman actually agreed to make this movie?

The doctor sticks his fingers in and around and kind of stretches her out. We see the top of the baby's head. Oh my God, it's huge!

I sit mesmerized as this woman pants and pushes and groans. It takes about thirty minutes, but finally the baby's head slides out, and the doctor suctions the baby's nose and mouth, and then tells the mother to give one more big push. The baby slides out all the way with a squelch, and the class actually cheers.

I let out the breath I'd been holding, and a tear glides down my cheek.

That was the most amazing, wonderful, miraculous thing I've ever seen.

Class is dismissed, and Martika hugs me close to her side as we walk to the car.

"What did you think?" she says. "I'm proud of you, that you watched it."

"Will you let me watch when it's your turn?" I ask.

Martika stops walking, pulls away, and looks at me. "Are you sure?"

"I won't look," I say. "I mean, I won't look straight on—"

She throws her arms around me. "It would mean so much to me," she says. "And I'm not embarrassed. You know that."

"If I can't experience it myself," I say, "I want to experience it with you."

Chapter 9

I do another show at the Ugly Mug and collect more names for my not-yet-existent newsletter. When I get home and check my messages, I find Martika's left two.

"Don't get on the Internet, okay?" she says. "Just trust me. Let's do coffee in the morning."

"Just making sure you're going straight to bed. It'll be better coming from me."

I can't ignore that.

So I fire up my laptop and put my name in the search engine.

"Joe Cruz's daughter is expecting! Her lesbian love child is due this spring!"

Say what?

They know I went to that class, and they think Martika is my lover! Ha, ha, ha, ha, ha!

It's funny. So not something to get worked up about.

So I go to bed.

☙

"Twenty-eight weeks pregnant!" Benny announces when I come through their door. "We're in the third trimester!"

I give him a hug. "So exciting!"

Martika comes in from the bedroom, still in her robe.

"Are you feeling okay?" I ask.

She nods. "I'm just exhausted. I barely slept. My legs keep jumping."

"Restless leg syndrome," Benny says. "I'm gonna have her take a hot bath after this and see if she can get a nap."

I sit next to her on the couch and rub her back. "I can go. You rest."

"No," she says. "I'm fine. We need to talk."

"I already saw it," I say. "So you're having my lesbian love child, huh?"

She smiles. "Is that all you saw?"

"There's more?"

Martika sighs. "There's a quote in one of the articles. From Matt."

I cock my head. "Matt?"

Benny brings her laptop over to us, and Marti finds the article in question. She reads, "Matt Russell, Cruz's ex-husband, only had one thing to say about her bisexuality. 'Hope can't have kids of her own, and she and Martika have been close since junior high.'"

I swipe the laptop out of her hands and read it for myself.

"Why would he tell someone that?" I whisper. "It's nobody's business."

"I'm sorry, Hope," Martika says.

I stare at the screen. None of what Matt said is a lie, but it makes me feel icky, like I'm standing naked in front of a crowd.

"Are you mad?" she asks.

I shake my head. "I'm...baffled. Matt knows I wouldn't want him saying anything about this. And if a reporter did corner him, and asked about my visit to that Lamaze class with you, this isn't the right response. He would have said that my best friend is pregnant and I must have been helping out. I mean, why go to the part about me not having kids of my own?"

"That must not be what the reporter asked," she says. "Maybe they flat-out told him we're lovers."

I laugh. "Matt would never believe that."

Martika frowns. "So...you're okay with this?"

I stand. "I'll ask him about it. That's all I can do." I bend forward and plant a kiss on her head. "Bye, Lover."

ℂ

So I head to the university. Matt should be on campus right now, and I want to catch him off guard so he can't prepare a lie.

My body itches as I think this. While not particularly forthcoming, Matt's never been a liar. But this breach of trust has me doubting him. And I hate that I feel that way about him.

Oh, wait. He cheated on me. He did lie, even if it was only one time. How quickly I've forgotten.

I head down the hall to his office. His door is open. I walk in to find him sitting at his desk, a youngish beauty draped over his shoulder. Both their laughter stops and the girl straightens up when I enter.

"I need a word in private," I say.

The girl looks at Matt. He stands too quickly, awkwardly. "Uh…Hope, this is Hailey. Hailey, Hope."

Hailey raises an eyebrow. She obviously knows who I am.

"We're still on for lunch, right?" she asks.

"I'll call you," he says.

Hailey frowns and exits, careful not to brush me on the way out.

"What happened to your hair?" Matt says. "Have a seat."

"Why did you tell a reporter that I'm unable to have kids?" I ask without sitting.

He blinks. "I didn't."

"You're quoted in the article," I say. "Seems a long shot that someone would guess that outta the blue."

"I would never have said that, Hope. You know me better than that."

"Did you speak to a reporter?" I ask.

He scrubs a hand through his hair. "One of them approached me in front of the house. But I didn't say anything about anything."

"What did you say?"

"Fuck off, if memory serves."

"Then how would they know?" I ask. "The only people that know are you, Martika and Benny, my ex who's still in China, and my mother. None of them would talk."

"Maybe your ex did," he says.

"No. Never."

Matt narrows his eyes. "So a guy you knew for a couple of months...you have more trust in him than you do in me?"

"He didn't cheat on me," I say.

"Right. He only left with no explanation."

I grit my teeth. I'm gonna have to tell Benny to shut the hell up.

"He's in China," I say. "There's no way it was him."

"Who knows who your mother's told," he says. "She speaks without thinking."

True. "But they attributed the quote to you. Why would they do that?"

Matt shrugs. "I don't know what to tell you. Either you believe me or you don't."

"I want to," I say. "But I think that would be naïve."

And I turn around and walk out.

Chapter 10

That Lamaze class movie lit something inside of me. Most likely, I'll never have a biological child of my own. But I want to grow something and take care of it.

I debate getting a pet. But I'm not at home that often, and I'm not certain I'm responsible enough. So instead, I decide on a vegetable garden.

I've never grown plants before. Sure, I have a yard, but I also have a gardener. I've never done the work myself.

I have a 10-foot-by-20-foot plot that runs along the back of the house. It has some random bushes in it, but if I clear those out, I'll have plenty of room to grow my own salad.

So I put some old clothes on and head to the yard. I grip the first bush and yank.

Nothing. This sucker must be in there pretty deep.

So I squat in the dirt and grab the main trunk close to the ground. The thorny leaves scratch my cheeks, but I grit my teeth, close my eyes, and pull. Puuuuulllll!

Nothing except some scratches on my palms. I need gloves.

Of course, I have no gloves except for some leather ones from my annual trips to New York with Mom. I can't ruin those. So I grab my oven mitts.

This is genius. The mitts even cover my forearms and save me from the pokey leaves. So I try again to pull the damn bush from the ground. I manage to strip an entire branch of leaves off, but that's it.

Maybe I can cut the bush down to size.

I grab a pair of scissors.

I spend two hours snipping whatever the scissors will cut through. Which is not much. But I do manage to denude the bush of all the leaves.

Hee, hee. I have a naked bush.

※

With my bank account $500 lighter, I come home from the hardware store with a shovel, a pickaxe, giant tree clippers, a supposedly-easy-to-install drip watering system, a long hose with a special spray nozzle, fertilizer, ten bags of mulch, an orange tree, a lemon tree, some bible about gardening in the West, and about 20 packets of seeds.

I'm getting serious.

I wrap a bandana around my blue head and grip the shovel tight. I thrust it as hard as I can near the base of the bush.

It goes about half an inch into the dirt.

So I put a foot on the shovel and try to push it in.

Nope.

I stand on the shovel. I jump on it. Not working.

I spend an hour scraping at the dirt.

This is ridiculous! I can't be this weak, or this stupid. How the hell does a gardener do this?

I need to make the dirt easier to dig. Maybe if I watered it…

I set the hose on high and put it at the base of the bush. Then I go make a pitcher of lemonade and turn on HGTV.

I wake up two hours later, a pool of drool under my cheek. I didn't realize gardening was so tiring.

The dirt should be good and watered by now. So I go out to the yard…holy crap! My backyard is a lake!

I splish splash through the water and turn off the hose. Water oozes into my shoes and I feel my toes getting squishy. I spy the edge of something yellow under the water and realize that all of my purchases are under three inches of water.

Even the seed packets.

My entire mission was to grow something and lovingly take care of it. I cannot let these seeds die!

So I scoop everything out of the mud and set it on the dry patio.

It takes me two hours, but I manage to dig up two of those bushes.

Then I literally sit my ass in the mud as the sun sets and dig rows of holes. I plant my seeds.

And I say a prayer that they take root.

Chapter 11

My phone rings, and caller ID says Alec Chang & Associates. A wave of anger rolls through me, and I almost don't answer. But I miss Alec. I'm worried about him.

"Hello?" I say tentatively.

"Is this Ms. Russell?" a female voice says.

"Yes."

"This is Wendy Brae with Alec Chang and Associates. Is this a good time?"

"Sure," I say, breathing a sigh of relief and feeling a pang of disappointment at the same time.

"I have the paperwork ready for your estate," she says. "Mr. Chang passed it along to me, and I'd like to set up a time to go over it with you. Would you like to come into the office, or is it easier if I come to you?"

"I can come in," I say. "I'm free now."

"Great," she says. "Mr. Chang insisted that I make you a top priority. I'll be here."

"I'm leaving now," I say.

80

I'm looking forward to this. I'm finally going to give my mother the things from my dad that she deserves, and I can stop feeling guilty for controlling her financially.

Ms. Wendy Brae doesn't keep me waiting. I don't even have time to sit before she appears, giving me a warm handshake and a smile.

"It's wonderful to finally meet you," she says. "Let's go back to my office."

I follow Ms. Brae's lead, and I can see Alec's office at the end of the hall. The door is open and the light is on.

I clear my throat. "Is Mr. Chang back from China?" I ask softly.

She nods. "He got back last week. Shall we say hello?"

I shake my head. "Maybe after."

She goes through the paperwork with me, and everything is in line with the plan Alec and I already discussed. My mother will be getting the two houses in LA that generate about $25,000 a month in rent, I'm setting up a trust account to pay for management and maintenance of the homes, and then I'm giving her $5 million in cash to do with as she sees fit.

I sign everything and thank Ms. Brae.

"Let me call Mr. Chang and have him come in," she says, reaching for her phone.

"No!" I say a little too loudly, and then I force myself to smile. "No. I'll just stop by his office on my way out."

I exit to the hallway and stare down in Alec's direction.

He's been home a week, and he didn't call me.

I don't have to see him. I can just leave.

"Is everything alright?" Ms. Brae asks as I stand shaking outside her office.

I smile at her. "Fine. Sorry. Thanks again."

And I force my feet to move.

☙

Have you ever seen that movie, *Poltergeist?* Scared the crap out of me as a kid, and there's a scene near the end where the mother is running down the hallway, trying to rescue her daughter from the ghosts, and the hallway gets longer and longer, and the more she runs, the farther away she is, and no matter how much she runs she can't get to the end…

That's what this is like. This fucking hallway stretches to forever.

But finally I'm there, at his door. I take a deep breath, knock on the jamb, and stick my head in. "Alec?"

He lifts his head at the sound of my voice, and he looks…tired. His eyes register pain that he doesn't hide quickly enough, but he plasters a small smile on his lips and stands.

"Hope."

I step into the doorway. "Hey. You're back."

He nods. "Did Wendy handle everything properly?"

"Why did you leave?" I blurt out.

Alec sighs.

He comes around his desk and shuts the door. We're standing a foot apart, and my heart pounds uncomfortably.

He waves me to a chair and we both sit.

"How have you been?" he asks.

"I'm not leaving until you tell me why you left."

Alec stares hard at his desk.

"It's long and complicated," he says, "but basically, my ex-wife returned to China to live with her parents about two months before I filed for divorce. We got married in China, but since I'm not a Chinese citizen, I could file for divorce here, and I did. She didn't contest it. Everything went through."

He takes a deep breath.

"But she was pregnant, Hope."

"You knew she was pregnant and you let her go?" I cry.

He shakes his head. "Of course I didn't know! She didn't tell me! But meanwhile, she contested our divorce in the Chinese courts, and I didn't know that, either. And then...I got a call from her mother. My wife was in a car accident and was in a coma. Her parents had been taking care of my daughter, but since it looked like my wife was about to die…they were going to put my daughter up for adoption."

I stare at him, but he still won't look at me.

"How could they do that?" I whisper.

He finally lifts his eyes to mine. "I had to go get her. I had to see to my wife. She died two weeks ago."

A tear slips down my cheek. "Did you bring your…daughter here?" I ask.

He nods. "She's eight months old."

I fight to keep my voice steady. "Why couldn't you tell me this?"

"I was still married, Hope," he says. "Technically. I was still responsible for her. If she'd survived, or was permanently disabled…it was my responsibility. I couldn't do that to you."

"I'm so sorry, Alec," I say. "That you had to go through that."

"You're not angry at me?" he asks. "That I was still married?"

I gape at him. "That's what you're hung up on? You didn't know, so no, I'm not mad at you for that. But I'm still mad."

"I didn't know how it would end," he says. "If it would end. I still care about you, Hope."

"Not enough to call and tell me you were back," I say with a forced laugh. "I care about you, too. And I know part of this was my fault. I had so little faith in myself...I guess it's not surprising that you had so little in me, too." I stand up. "Take care of yourself, Alec."

Chapter 12

Martika invites me over for dinner, saying she has something important to discuss. And I have something important to discuss with her, too. What should I do about Alec?

She gives me a hug at the door. "Is Benny working?" I ask. "I noticed his car's gone."

Martika nods as we head to the kitchen. She grabs a big bowl of salad and sets it on the kitchen table, and I grab the pitcher of iced tea from the fridge. I pour us both a glass while she sits.

"Benny's being deployed," she says, and I pause mid-pour.

"When?"

"Three days," she says, her voice breaking. I watch her blink hard.

"Oh, honey." I set down the pitcher and lean over her for a hug. She clings to me.

I pull away and carefully wipe the tears from her cheeks. "You're a warrior's wife, and you're a warrior yourself. We'll get through it."

She nods. "I know. I just...the baby changes everything. I've never worried about him before. I mean, not really. He's solid. The guys on his team are solid. But now...if something happens to him, Hope..."

I grab her hand and crouch down in front of her. "What do you need from me? Whatever you need, I'll do it."

She squeezes my hand. "You'll still go to Lamaze class with me, right?"

"Of course."

"And when I get closer to my due date, like a week away…will you stay here with me? Just in case?"

My eyes sting. "Of course."

"Will you be my lesbian lover?"

I blink. "Hell, no."

She laughs, and I join her.

"I'm here," I say. "I'll help you through it. You won't be alone."

"I knew that," she says. "I don't tell you enough, and maybe I've never told you at all, but…you're the best friend in the world, Hope."

That does it. Tears roll down my cheeks. "So are you, baby," I say. "So are you."

We eat, and Martika brings out Benny's many lists, and we go over the plan for the next couple of months. Damn, there's a lot to do to prepare for a baby.

Which makes me think of Alec. He didn't have nine months to prepare. He barely had time to get used to the idea, let alone get his life in order.

"I talked to Alec today," I say as we wash dishes.

Martika turns off the faucet and raises an eyebrow. "He called you?"

I shake my head. "I saw him at his office when I went there to sign stuff. He got back last week and didn't tell me."

"Did he explain?" she asks.

I tell her the story, and we both sigh as we sink to the couch.

"So what are you going to do?" she asks.

I shrug. "I still love him. But I don't know if there's anything I can do."

"You can tell him that you still love him," she says. "Tell him you still want to be with him."

"I don't know if I do," I say.

Martika wrinkles her brow. "Why wouldn't you?" There's anger in her voice.

"Why are you mad?"

She shifts on the couch. "You're throwing away something really good. And why? What are you afraid of?"

I gape at her. "Afraid of? This doesn't have anything to do with fear. He left me, Marti. He left without even giving me an explanation. He didn't trust that I could handle it. Is that the kind of relationship that's good for me?"

"Hope, you have to be honest with yourself," she says. "We don't know if you could have handled it. You have these weird breakdowns, and you don't even have confidence in yourself—"

"You have confidence in me," I say. "You're counting on me to help you with this pregnancy. You didn't question me…did you?"

She shakes her head. "Never. But we've known each other practically our whole lives. Alec's only known you a few months. What if his wife had survived? He was saving you from something really painful."

"It was painful either way," I say. "He should have been honest with me."

"He should have," she concedes. "But nobody's perfect. You're asking him to deal with your flaws, but you're refusing to deal with his."

I sit back and close my eyes. She's right.

"Maybe it won't work out anyway," she says. "Who knows? But do you want to regret not trying? Alec is worth trying for. Isn't he?"

Chapter 13

Magician Martika manages to throw together a going-away party for Benny in two days. He's leaving in the morning out of Coronado.

This party is completely different than the last one they had. It's quiet, somber almost, as people whisper in small groups. Everyone fights to get time alone with Ben.

Then there's Benny's family, his mother weeping in the corner while his sisters comfort her. Martika spends some time with her mother-in-law, but then she drags me to the bathroom and locks us in.

"I can't handle this," she says, leaning on the counter. "Ben doesn't need his last memory at home to be of his wailing mother."

"He knows how she is," I say. "It's always been this way with her."

"But I've never been pregnant before!" she whispers furiously. "I don't need this!"

"And Benny doesn't need you hysterical, too," I say. "Buck up, little camper."

Martika cracks a smile at that. "Thank God my mom's not here. She'd be yelling at Ben for leaving."

"Mothers are crazy," I say. "There's a lesson here, you know that?"

She hangs head. "Dear God, I'm gonna be like them, aren't I?"

"I don't see you crying during a family party, but I could see you yelling at your daughter-in-law. Definitely something to guard against in the future."

Martika gives me a brief hug and steels her spine. "Okay, I'm better now."

We hear the doorbell ring.

"Oh," she says. "That might be for you."

I raise an eyebrow. "What did you do?"

She smiles and opens the door. We walk out to the foyer, and there's Ben, holding the front door open, and Charles standing on the steps.

"Charles!" I yell, and I run to him.

He laughs as I crush him in a hug. "I was hoping you'd be here tonight," he says, planting a kiss on the top of my head.

I look up at him. He's just as handsome as I remembered. "Did you just get in?"

He nods. "I couldn't miss this. Had to share a beer with my oldest friend before he goes off to protect us."

I step back. "Have your time with him. We can catch up later."

Charles gives me a soft kiss. "I'm counting on it."

As Charles walks away with Ben, I look up. Alec is standing in the doorway.

"Alec!" Martika cries, edging around me and taking his hand. "It's so nice of you to come!"

He kisses her cheek, but his eyes are on me. "Thanks for inviting me."

My head whips to Martika at that, but she refuses to look at me.

"Come on in," she says. "Hope can help you get something to drink." Then she rushes out to the patio, leaving us standing there.

"I guess you didn't know she invited me," Alec says.

"Martika likes surprises," I say.

"Do you like surprises?" he asks.

I ignore the question. "What are you doing here?"

"I was invited," he says.

"And?"

He looks around. "Is this the appropriate time? Honestly, I thought we could hang out and maybe talk later. But it seems like your later is occupied."

"Charles is an old friend," I say. "That's it."

"An old boyfriend?"

Well…we slept together the first night we met, and it was magical, but he lives in Texas. We've kept in touch, but that's it.

"Not really," I say.

Alec shakes his head. "Enough. I can't be upset. I broke things off. But the unfortunate part is…I want to fuck that guy up."

I laugh. Never thought I'd hear those words coming out of Alec's mouth.

"What are you doing here?" I say gently. "Really."

He blows out a breath. "I want another shot. I still love you, Hope."

My heart skips. "I don't know, Alec. You're right, this isn't the greatest time. But we can talk after."

His eyes soften. "You'll give me that time?"

I nod.

Alec opens his arms. I fall into them, and we hold each other tight.

And when I pull away and open my eyes…there's Matt standing at the door.

∞

I manage to corner Martika in the kitchen.

"Three of them," I say. "Three of them! Here. Tonight. Together!"

She sighs. "It's…awkward," she says. "I get it. But there's nothing we can do."

"But why did you have to invite all three of them?"

"I didn't," she says. "I let Charles know, but I never thought he'd show up. Ben invited Matt. Yes, I invited Alec, but that's only because you didn't have the guts to."

"Great," I say. "Blame me. Thanks a lot."

"It's fine," she says. "You and Matt know where you stand. Just be honest with Charles that you're seeing Alec. And then go home and screw Alec's brains out."

I throw back my Coke. "There's a plan."

Martika smiles. "See? Problem solved."

❧

Charles gives me a wave as I step out to the patio. I sit next to him on a bench, and he mashes his thigh into mine.

"Is something wrong?" he asks.

I smile. "How do you know that? You know me that well?"

He shrugs. "Those two guys are eyeing you, and you're trying too hard not to eye them back."

I bump my shoulder into his. "The big one is my ex-husband. And the other is a recent ex-boyfriend. And then there's you. Unfortunately…I have feelings for all of you."

"Shit," he says. "Guess you have some decisions to make. But I won't make it harder for you. I know you don't want a long-distance relationship."

"I don't," I say, "but I want us to stay friends."

Charles grins. "I'm a great friend."

℘

When I return from using the bathroom for real, I see Matt…talking to Alec. They both notice me and ignore me.

Shit.

So I hang out with Martika and Benny.

Benny's family finally leaves, and then Charles and a few other friends follow. Charles invites me out for drinks with the group, but I decline.

Matt tears himself away from Alec, and asks me if I'll show him out. I follow him to his car, and I'm dying to ask what he and Alec talked about, but I don't. How desperate would that make me sound?

We reach his car, and Matt palms his keys.

"I promised Ben I'd look out for Martika," he says. "I know you'll be the one here with her, so if you need anything, call me, okay?"

I nod. "Thanks. I will."

"This really sucks for them, doesn't it?"

"That's putting it mildly, I think," I say.

"You're gonna be an aunt," he says. "Exciting, isn't it?"

"I haven't thought about the baby much," I admit. "I'm more worried about getting Martika through it."

"That's why she's lucky to have you."

I smile at that. "Thanks, Matt."

He kisses my cheek. "Now go talk to Alec," he says. "The guy's dying."

ഇ

Alec and Ben are laughing when I return. Martika is cleaning up.

"Let me help," I say, but she shakes her head.

"Get out of here. Go be with Alec. I want some alone time with my husband."

I head to the patio and stop in front of the guys. "Time for me to wish you a safe journey."

Benny gives me a tight hug, the tightest, and I whisper a prayer in his ear.

"Vaya con Díos," I say, giving him one last kiss on the ear.

Alec shakes his hand, and then takes mine and leads me out to our cars.

"How late is your babysitter prepared to stay?" I ask him as we stand awkwardly in the street.

"She's staying with Auntie Ju-Ju overnight," Alec says.

"She…what's her name?" I ask.

"Mei," he says.

"Mei. That's beautiful."

He smiles. "She is."

I smile back. "My place or yours?"

"Let's meet at mine."

Chapter 14

Alec's house looks like a toy store exploded. My head swivels around, taking in the mess, and then I step on something that squeaks. A stuffed duck. I pick the duck up and hold it to my chest.

"Guess you've been a little overwhelmed," I say.

He laughs. "There's not enough time in the day. I'm still learning, and I haven't quite got our routine down yet. You want a beer?"

I didn't drink at the party. I wanted to be clear-headed for Martika. But now, I definitely need a drink.

"Please."

He grabs us each one, and we sit on the couch, not touching.

"So why didn't I tell you I was back?" he asks. "That's the big question, isn't it?"

"One of them," I say.

"First there was shame," he says, his eyes on his bottle. "Shame that I had a failing wife, that I was still married, that I didn't know I had a daughter. I physically couldn't tell you what was happening. My body wouldn't let me."

My initial reaction is that this is an excuse. But I've had moments where I wanted to say something and couldn't. My mouth simply wouldn't work.

I nod.

"Then...she might have lived. My wife might have survived. And even though I'd done everything I could think of to help her...I was obligated to do more. I didn't want you involved in that. And then...I knew I still wanted to be with you. But I didn't want you to think I just needed help. I was hoping to get a handle on everything, and figure out how to be a good father and still get to work on time...I needed to do all of that before I talked to you. I don't want you here out of pity, or because I have a baby. I want you here because you love me and only me."

"I would have stuck by you," I say.

Alec nods. "I know that. It wasn't about you. It was about me, and what I was feeling. It was about what I needed to do. And I know that hurt you, Hope. I'm so sorry for that."

"Like you said...we moved fast," I say. "We haven't had time to share everything, but all these things have been happening, and it's made us look like we haven't been honest, but that's not it at all. We just don't know each other yet."

He takes a deep breath. "I want to. I want us to know each other, inside and out."

"Me, too," I say. "That time without you...it was awful."

Alec smiles at that. "Awful, huh?"

"Awful."

"What about Matt?"

I cock my head. "What about him?"

"Do you still have feelings for him?"

I pick at the label on my bottle. "He was such a huge part of my life for so long," I say. "I think I'll always care about him. But I don't want to be with him."

"So how do we do this?" he asks.

I almost say, "I'll be whatever you need." Because, clearly, Alec has the tougher life right now.

But I catch myself.

"Let's date," I say. "Let's continue to get to know each other. And we'll see how it goes from there."

Alec nods. "I've missed you. We have until eight in the morning. That's when Auntie Ju-Ju is dropping Mei off."

I scoot up close to him. "And what do you do with Mei while you work?"

"I have a nanny."

"You need to tell her to clean up."

Alec smiles. "If it's a choice between spending time with Mei or cleaning up, I choose time with Mei."

"Sensible."

Alec puts his hands on my cheeks. "Kiss me already, will you?"

☙

I'm out of the house at seven. I told Alec I had an early appointment.

Which I do if you count eleven o'clock as early.

I just didn't want to see Auntie Ju-Ju so early in the morning when it was obvious I spent the night.

Okay, okay. So I'm a little nervous about meeting Mei, too.

I don't know how to hold a baby. I don't know how to change a diaper. Alec will see what an incompetent mother I'd be, and he'll want nothing more to do with me.

I wonder how long I can put him off.

Chapter 15

I put my music on the back burner, and I rearrange my life to help Martika. Not that I had much of a life to rearrange, let's be honest. Sunday activities with my mother, Wednesday nights playing at the coffeehouse until they get tired of me...that's pretty much the extent of my schedule.

Now I have Monday night Lamaze class, Tuesday night parenting class, and—at Martika's urging—Thursday morning workouts with a trainer.

It had to be done.

My trainer's name is Sadie, and she was in the Navy with Martika. Enough said.

We spend the first session getting a handle on my current fitness level. Sadie puts me through the paces, trying to determine where I'm weak. I could have saved us a lot of time by telling her "everywhere."

"It's not as bad as you think," she says as I throw myself on the floor and run a towel over my face. "Arm strength needs work, but your cardio's decent."

"I've had some pretty good sex lately," I say, and we both laugh.

"Sex is great exercise," she says. "And it's good for your relationship, too. I recommend once a day."

"My boyfriend will love to hear that," I say.

She pulls me to my feet. "You're gonna be sore, but you have to work through it. Do the arm exercises I showed you three times a week. Light cardio four times a week. We'll start slow and add stuff over time."

"That's starting slow?" I ask.

Sadie grins. "Yes, this is slow. I want to hear from your doctor before I really push you."

Right. My appointment's tomorrow afternoon.

"Drink lots of water," she says, "and call me if you have any questions."

Right.

⊗

Alec offered to come to the appointment with me, but I opted for Martika. Whatever the news about my heart—if there is any news—I want some time to think about how to tell him.

I've known Dr. Parsa for fifteen years. She greets me with a hug. "Where's that gorgeous husband of yours?" she asks.

"This is my best friend, Martika," I say. "Matt and I divorced last year."

Dr. Parsa grabs my hand. "Hope, I'm so sorry."

"Thank you," I say. "It was tough for a while, but I'm good now."

"Then let's take a look," she says. "The nurse said you're not experiencing any negative symptoms?"

I shake my head. "Nope. No pain, no shortness of breath."

"Let me look at the echocardiogram we did."

Martika and I sit patiently while she examines my test results.

Dr. Parsa finally looks up and smiles. "Everything looks good, Hope. No changes from last year. Are you getting much exercise?"

"I just hired a trainer," I say. "The focus is gonna be on my physical strength, but I'd like to do more cardio, too. Can I?"

She nods. "You should. There's no need to push yourself to the max, but a few times a week where you get your heart pumping is great. Like I said, don't push it. Listen to your body. If you feel out of breath, stop."

"I do have one other question," I say. "I know in the past, you've recommended that I don't get pregnant. But if I did…if it's something I really wanted…"

Her eyes soften and she takes my hand. "I thought you'd decided not to have kids."

"That's what Matt and I had decided," I say, "but Matt's gone."

She rolls her stool over to me and sits down. "It would be a high-risk pregnancy. I can't predict how your heart will take it. Everything might be fine, or it might strain your valve to the point where you need a replacement. But you will need a replacement at some point. I've told you that. The fix you had at birth…nothing lasts forever. This is really something you need to discuss with your partner, Hope."

"I don't mean to be rude," Martika says, "but that wasn't very helpful. She knew all that."

I cringe and swat Martika's arm, and Dr. Parsa sighs. "Many patients with your condition have successful pregnancies. The mechanical valves today are much better than the valves of ten years ago, even five years ago. Our surgical procedures are better. Right now, I'd say you're an excellent candidate for pregnancy. You don't even have a heart murmur. But there are no guarantees. I can't make the choice for you, Hope."

Tears gather in my eyes. "You think I'm an excellent candidate to have a baby?"

She smiles. "As far as your heart goes, yes."

"What's that supposed to mean?" Martika asks.

Dr. Parsa narrows her eyes. "You will have health issues, Hope. You have health issues. You can't just think in terms of having a baby. You'll need a strong support system, ideally a strong, committed partner. If you choose to get pregnant, I'd want all of us working together—me, your neurologist, your OB/GYN, a mental healthcare provider. From beginning to end, we should all be involved."

"I'm finally seeing a psychiatrist," I say. "He's really helping me."

"Excellent. And do you have a partner?"

I nod. "It's new, and he knows about my heart, and we haven't actually discussed getting pregnant, but I wanted to know my options."

Dr. Parsa gives me a hug. "You're doing the right things. Take care of yourself, and keep me in the loop."

ഔ

"So what do you think?" Martika asks when we get in the car.

"I can't think," I say. "It doesn't seem real."

Martika shifts to face me. "This is something you really need to think about, front to back. I mean, I'm happy for you, so happy...but there are consequences."

I nod as I drive. "I know. I'm not gonna run off and get pregnant."

"And you should tell Alec everything the doctor said—"

"I will," I say, feeling a little irritated.

"You should talk to Dr. Steinburg about this," she presses. "Like she said, all your doctors should be involved—"

"I get it!" I turn and glare at her. "Why are you up my ass about this?"

"I'm not up your ass," she says. "I just want you to think hard about this and do the right thing."

"And what do you think the right thing is?" I ask.

Martika stays silent.

"Well? You seem to know what's best for me. What should I do?"

"Hope."

"Don't Hope me," I say. "You don't think I should have a baby, do you?"

"I never said that."

"But that's what you think, isn't it?"

We pull up to her house, and Marti pushes her door open then looks back at me. "Aren't you coming in?"

I shake my head. "I should go."

"Please, Hope," she says. "Please come inside."

I sigh, turn the car off, and march inside. "What do you want?" I ask her.

I follow her to the kitchen, where she picks a manila folder up off the counter and hands it to me.

"Ben and I had Alec create a trust for us, with a will and stuff," she says. "We'd been meaning to do it, but it's not like we have any assets beyond the house, and even that's mortgaged to the hilt. But when he got called back out, Ben's first thought was that we needed to protect the baby, just in case."

I open the folder.

"It's on page four," she says, and I flip to page four.

I blink hard as I read, then my eyes whip to hers. "You named me guardian of the baby?"

Martika nods. "If you'll do it."

"But you have family, both of you. One of your sisters, your moms...they'll never let me—"

"It's not up to them," she says. "It's up to me and Benny."

"They'll fight it," I say. "I have too many health problems."

"But you have enough money to fight them," she says. "And we spoke with Alec and several people in his office, and they all know our wishes. We're trusting you with the thing that matters most to us."

I choke on a sob. "You think I'll be a good mother."

She smiles and takes my hands in hers. "I know you'll be a great mother. But...should you get pregnant? I don't know, Hope. I don't want to lose you. I don't know if it's worth the risk. But I want you to know that my opinion has nothing to do with your ability to be a good mom. That's a given."

Chapter 16

Alec invites me over for dinner to meet Mei, and since it's been two weeks since we started dating again, I know I can't continue to hide. I decide to just come clean.

"Um…you know I've never been around babies, right?"

"Is that why you've been avoiding coming over here?" he asks.

"Well…yeah. I'm nervous."

Alec laughs. "Don't be. I'll help. I'm not exactly a pro myself. Plus, this is great opportunity to be ready for Martika's baby, right?"

"I guess," I say. "Okay. What should I bring?"

"An overnight bag," he says, voice low. "And that massage oil. I can use a massage."

I laugh. "Okay. See you soon."

ഗ

I can hear Mei wailing as I walk up to the front door. Oh boy.

I can do this.

I take a deep breath and open the door. "Alec?"

He's pacing in front of the couch, clutching a sobbing bundle of blankets to his shoulder. "Just in time."

I smile. "I don't know that I'll be much help."

"If you can take her for five minutes while I heat a bottle, I'll love you forever."

I close the door and walk over to them. "Hey, Mei."

The baby doesn't seem to notice me. She's got herself all worked up, her face scrunched and her lungs bursting.

"What's wrong with her?" I ask.

Alec bounces on his toes. "Who knows? Sometimes babies just cry. I haven't figured out a surefire way to soothe her yet. I'm hoping a bottle will help."

He lifts Mei into my shaking arms, and I hold her tight to my chest. "Hey, you."

She cries harder.

"Oh, let's not cry," I say, shifting her up to my shoulder. I bounce around the room. "I want to meet you. I want to talk to you. My name's Hope. I love your daddy, you know that?"

I watch Alec fumble with a bottle. His sink is full of dirty dishes, the counter, too, and he seems completely off balance.

"It's okay," I say to him with a laugh. "Take a breather. I've got her."

He puts his hands on the counter and leans forward. "She's been crying for an hour. Makes you feel like shit."

"Then get the bottle and grab a beer. Or go for a walk. Seriously, I'm fine."

He smiles at me and continues with the bottle. "I wouldn't leave you here alone, but I appreciate the offer."

"Does she like you to sing to her?" I ask.

"You've heard me sing," he says. "I'm pretty sure me singing would be considered child abuse." He comes out of the kitchen and holds out his arms. "I'll feed her."

I pluck the bottle from his hand. "Get a beer. I'm doing this."

I settle on the couch and move a squirming Mei to my lap. I try to give her the bottle, but she wriggles around and pushes it away.

"I prefer a little entertainment with my dinner, too," I say. And then I sing *Twinkle, Twinkle, Little Star.*

At first, Mei screams louder, seemingly in an effort to drown me out. And then she hiccoughs. She turns her bright brown eyes on me and blinks.

I sing softer, and I bring the bottle back to her lips.

She sniffles, then opens her mouth, and her tiny hands help guide the bottle in.

Bingo.

Alec comes to the couch with two beers, and he sits right up next to me.

"You're a genius," he whispers.

A tear glides down my cheek.

I watch this beautiful little girl fall asleep with her fingers wrapped around my pinkie. My heart is so full it feels ready to burst.

❧

"You're always so hard on yourself," Alec says as we eat pizza on the living room floor. "When are you going to start believing in yourself?"

I take a bite of my crust. "How can I be confident in something I've never done? This baby thing is uncharted territory."

"Didn't look that way to me," he says.

I duck my head. "She's precious," I say. "You're so blessed."

Alec sighs and rolls to his back. "She's got me. I'd do anything for her. But I'd be lying if I said it was easy."

"It's still new," I say. "But you're lucky. You have lots of family to help out."

He flips over to his stomach and props his head in his hands. "How does this change things for us?"

"It makes it a lot more serious, doesn't it?" I say. "I mean, we have Mei to think about. Whatever happens between us will affect her, too."

Alec nods. "Is that a problem?"

I shrug. "You and I have always been serious."

"But?"

I throw my crust in the pizza box. "What if I get close to Mei, and then you and I don't work out? What then?"

"It's the same as getting married, having kids, and then divorcing," he says. "There's always the possibility of disaster. But we can't assume disaster."

"Except that if Mei were really mine, I'd still get to see her. Now...I have no claim to her. I'm already falling in love with her, and there are no guarantees."

Alec sits up and pulls me into his chest. "What do you want, Hope?"

I look into his eyes. "I want us to work out. And I guess we just have to take a leap of faith."

He leans in and kisses me, but I pull back. "What do you want, Alec?"

"You," he says. "I just want you."

I smile and kiss his nose. "Come on. I'll help you clean the kitchen. There's no way I can have a satisfying orgasm until the work is done."

Alec laughs and pops to his feet.

છ

We share a lazy morning, coffee, news, and Mei. Alec surrounds her with pillows in the middle of the floor and encourages her to sit up by herself.

He has a book that tells you all the milestones a baby is supposed to hit every month. I flip to the section on "Eight Months Old," and it says that most babies are crawling or scooting, and they should be able to sit up.

"Have you read this?" I ask him as he sits a falling Mei up again. "She should be able to sit up on her own."

He nods. "Her gross motor skills are behind the curve. Her pediatrician said there's nothing physically wrong with her. Most likely, she was in a crib all day and didn't get a lot of opportunity to use her muscles. He thinks she'll catch up quickly."

I read some more. "And you should be introducing new foods to her. One a week."

"She'd never eaten solid foods except for rice cereal," he says. "We're doing peas this week."

"Peas?" I say, scrunching my nose. "You want her to like vegetables. Why start with peas?"

"The doctor suggested it. He said to start with the green vegetables, otherwise she won't touch them at all. Carrots and squash and everything not green are much sweeter."

"Damn, babies are smart," I say. "It says she should know a few words. Does she talk yet?"

"She can say 'Ma.' I've been trying to get her to say 'Da.'"

I sit in front of her and smile. "Dada. That's your Dada. Can you say Dada? Dada."

Mei blows a raspberry at me and laughs.

"I wonder if this is confusing for her," I say. "She's used to hearing Chinese, not English."

Alec pulls me up into his arms. "I love that you're concerned about her."

"Of course I am," I say. "It doesn't sound like she got the best start." He kisses me, and I pull back. "Do you think we should be doing that in front of her?"

Alec laughs. "I think it's good for her to see people being affectionate. I didn't have that, and I want her to have it."

"How is it that you're so affectionate if you didn't have it?"

He cocks his head. "How did you know it's wrong to hit your child?"

I close my eyes. "You just know, in your gut, when something feels wrong."

"Exactly."

I open my eyes. "So what was wrong with our parents?"

Alec pulls me back against him. "I guess we'll never know."

Chapter 17

Dr. Steinburg offers me a cup of coffee, and I take it. With Mei up twice last night, my ass is dragging.

"So why the yawning?" he asks as I try to discreetly cover my open mouth with my hand.

I tell him all about Alec and Mei.

"And then Alec and I were talking about how to raise kids, I mean, some things specifically, like he wants to show Mei a lot of affection since he didn't get that as a kid, and of course, I would never hit my child, and I just wondered...what was wrong with our parents? Why didn't they see they were hurting us?"

He sits back. "One reason is how they were raised. If, for example, you are hit as a child, you are more likely to hit your own children. And not because you think it's good or right, and not because you don't realize you're hurting them, but because that is what you were taught. That is how things are done. You lived through it, so your children will, too."

"But Alec and I will never repeat the abuse," I say. "Never. So why are we different?"

"In Alec's case, it's more a cultural difference," he says. "He was raised here, where hugging and kissing your child is pretty standard. And it sounds like he went through a marriage that didn't have a lot of affection, and since he's an intelligent man, he decided he wanted something different. With you, I think a big part of it is the absence of substance abuse. Both your parents spent decades in a drug-induced haze, and you are clear-headed. But beyond that…I'd say your relationship with Matt has a lot to do with it."

"One more thing I owe him for," I say.

Dr. Steinburg raises an eyebrow. "Has something happened between you two?"

"No," I say. "Well, you know we decided to just be friends, and he and Alec both showed up at a party and they got to talking…I have no idea what they actually talked about, but Matt sorta gave me his blessing to be with Alec. And I've been feeling guilty about that. I don't know why, though."

"I think you know you need to let go of the guilt," he says. "By having an affair, Matt was pretty much letting you off the hook for any imbalance in the relationship."

I blink. "He was letting me off the hook?"

"Subconsciously," he says. "He committed the greatest sin against you that he could live with. That way he was the bad guy. Even if he didn't realize what he was doing, it was very calculated."

"Why didn't you tell me this before?"

Dr. Steinburg eyes me over his coffee cup. "This information changes something for you?"

I shake my head. "I don't know. I just…I never thought of his affair as something that was actually motivated by his care for me."

"It was, and it wasn't. He wanted out, but he wanted to make it easy on you. You can't take this as a sign of love, Hope. That's not what I was getting at."

I nod.

"My point was about guilt. Let it go. Focus on Alec. How do you feel about him being a father?"

I try to focus on the question, but all I can think about is Matt, compromising himself, so I didn't have to feel bad.

"Wait. If Matt wanted to make it easy on me, he could have just left. He didn't have to have an affair."

Dr. Steinburg sighs. "This is more complex than I've made it. Matt needed to feel appreciated, according to what he told you. So he found that in a grad student. He was confused, he wasn't sure if he wanted out of the marriage…and then he told Benny about the affair, who told Martika, who told you. Why do you think he told Benny? He'd already gotten away with it. He wanted a way out without having to take responsibility, without having to say, Hope, I'm leaving because of you. Ultimately, he made you do the dirty work, and he got to wallow in his own guilt. Win, win."

"Men," I say, and he smiles.

"And they say women are the more complex gender. Let's go back to you and Alec. How did your cardiologist visit go?"

I pick at a hangnail. "I can have kids. She told me I can get pregnant."

"That's wonderful, Hope. How did Alec take it?"

"I haven't told him," I say. "And he didn't ask. But I don't blame him. He's completely overwhelmed right now."

"Do you intend to tell him?"

"Someday," I say. "I just...don't you think it's a lot of pressure right now? A year from now, my doctor might say it's not safe to have a baby. Hell, tomorrow it might not be safe. I don't want Alec to feel like I'm pushing him."

"I think that's wise," he says. "Are you feeling pressure yourself?"

"Of course," I say. "It's all I can think about. But then I spent time with Alec and Mei...I know it's not easy. And I know it's not something I want to do on my own, raise a kid, I mean. I want that perfect partner first."

"I agree. How goes the music?"

I tell him about Lady Strings, my new persona, and that it's coming along.

"Lady Strings," he says. "How'd you come up with that?"

"It's a nickname Matt gave me in high school," I say. "All my close friends called me Strings, although I made them stop when Matt and I separated."

Dr. Steinburg smiles.

"What?" I ask.

"You realize this means you're not really hiding. If more than one person knows, you'll be outed."

I smile back. "Yeah, I kinda figured that."

Chapter 18

I spend the night at Alec's again. I was worried about getting close to Mei too soon, but I just decided to jump.

We make love after Mei falls asleep, and I decide to jump further.

"I didn't tell you about my appointment with the cardiologist," I say.

"I forgot all about it," he says. "I'm so sorry. How'd it go?"

I smile. "Great. Everything's fine. And she...she even said...I can get pregnant."

His eyes widen. "Really? It's safe?"

I nod, and Alec pulls me down to his chest and wraps his arms around me.

"Wow. So what are you thinking?"

"Nothing," I say. "I don't want to screw this up. I don't want you to feel like I have to get pregnant. This doesn't change anything. Let's just keep going."

"Hope," he whispers, and the emotion in his voice makes me shiver. "I have to be honest with you."

I lift my head in alarm. "What?"

"This...Mei has changed everything for me, and I don't want to make any absolutes, but I...I think..."

"What?"

"I don't think I want any more children."

I sit up, too fast, and turn away from him.

"I don't know for sure," he says, "but I'm pretty sure."

"Do you think, maybe, you're just overwhelmed?" I say without looking at him.

"Probably," he says. "But that doesn't change anything. I can't imagine it'd be easier with more kids."

"But you're doing it all alone now," I say, my voice rising. "And if we ever…I mean, hypothetically, if we got married, we'd be doing it together."

"You were prepared to never have kids," he says, "and suddenly you're angry that I don't want more?"

"I'm not angry," I say. "Or maybe I am. I just…you're making a huge decision without even discussing it."

"Mei is one more child than you thought you'd ever have," he says. "You can't be happy with that?"

I climb from the bed and search for my clothes. "If Mei was all I ever had, yes, I'd be happy. But it's in God's hands. Whatever happens…I just want the chance for it to happen. And you're deciding for me."

"We have to agree, or one of us decides," he says. "If we don't agree, one of us has to compromise."

"I don't know if I can compromise on this," I say. "Not after I've been given a chance."

I pull on my jeans and shove my feet in my tennis shoes.

"Don't go," he says. "Nothing's changed. We haven't even decided to have a baby."

"But you've decided not to," I say. "Alec, I love you. I want a life with you. But if you're dead-set against this...neither of us should waste our time."

"I don't know what I want," he says quietly.

"There seems to be an epidemic of that running around. And I don't want to catch it. Goodbye, Alec."

To Be Continued…

BOOKS BY ANDREA RING

Stand-Alone Contemporary Romance

High Maintenance

Young Adult Contemporary Romance

Under Water (A Yellow Wood Series Book 1)

Breaking the Surface (A Yellow Wood Series Book 2)

Romantic Fantasy

The Go-Between (Nilaruna Cycles Book 1)

The Princess (Nilaruna Cycles Book 2)

Goddess (Nilaruna Cycles Book 3)

Science Fiction

Nervous System (The System Series Book 1)

Systematic (The System Series Book 2)

Operating System (The System Series Book 3)

Honor System (The System Series Book 4)

Systems Go (The System Series Book 5)

Note to my readers: I'm humbled and grateful that you read my work. I hope it touched you. I'd love to get to know you, hear your thoughts, and learn what makes you tick. Send me an email. Write a review on Amazon. Comment on my blog. You're the reason I write, and I'll never forget that.

Read a chapter from the next episode in The String Serial,

String Theory
The String Serial
Part Four

String Theory

I help Martika into the car after her doctor visit. She's clearly uncomfortable and trying not to show it.

I pull out of the parking lot, and she sighs.

"Okay. First thing I do is try to contact Benny. Then I need to pack my bag for the hospital. You have my list of contacts, right? All the people who need to be called when I go into labor?"

"Yes, dear," I say.

She rolls her eyes at me.

"We can finally put the sheets on the crib…and remind me to sleep with a towel under my butt. If my water breaks in the middle of the night, I don't want to deal with the clean up."

"Got it."

"Then a power walk. Three miles oughta do it. We can walk again after dinner."

I've lost five pounds in the last three weeks. Martika is on a mission to get this baby out as soon as possible.

"I can't believe you're already dilated two centimeters," I say. "With any luck, you'll be most of the way there before you're actually in pain. Nervous?" I ask.

She smiles. "No. I know I should be, but no. I can't believe it's finally here."

"She said you might still be a week away."

Martika shakes her head. "No way. Two days tops. My uterus is scrunching itself up as we speak."

I laugh. "It's your cervix that needs to do the work, not your uterus."

"Look at you," she says. "Miss Pregnancy Expert. Take a guess. When is this little guy coming?"

I reach a hand out and put it on her belly. "Tonight. After midnight. You're gonna wake me up, and we'll rush to the hospital, and he'll be here by sunrise."

"My son wouldn't be so rude as to interrupt my last night of rest. I say tomorrow morning. I wake up, my water breaks while I'm in the shower, I arrive at the hospital ten centimeters dilated, and I push for ten minutes, and boom. I'm a mama."

"You're dreaming," I say with a laugh.

About the Author

Andrea Ring was born and raised in Orange County, California. At age eight, she wrote an essay proclaiming she wanted to be an "auther" when she grew up. It only took her thirty years to realize her dream.

She enjoys beating her four children at Boggle, reading science fiction and fantasy, and eating bacon. She hates to exercise, but loves taking walks with her family through Old Towne Orange. She's lucky to be married to the love of her life.

She thinks every book should contain a love story.

Did we mention her love of bacon?